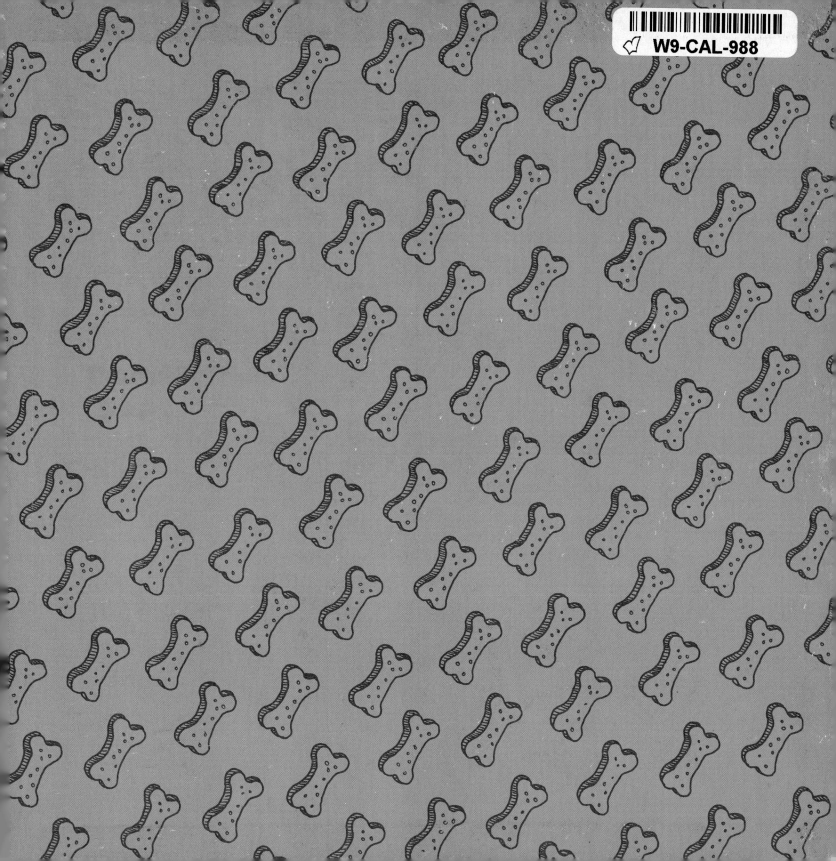

This book belongs to

Cody

Christmas 1998

Published by Bethany House Publishers under license from Bethel Publishing, publisher of
Spunky's Diary by Janette Oke. This story was adapted for television by Patrick Granleese and
modified for print by Sue & Lorianne Wilkinson. Illustrated by Elizabeth Gatt,
Sue Wilkinson, Holly Lennox & Ritchie Lebrun. Art Direction by Angela Ward Costello,
Sue Wilkinson & Dynomight Cartoons.

Library of Congress Cataloging-in-Publication Data
CIP Data applied for

Based on character and story by

JANETTE OKE

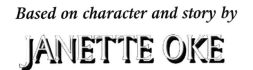

Spunky's™ First Christmas

Spunky has hidden his toy bone somewhere on each double page. Can you find it?

Spunky's eyes popped open, and his soft, floppy ears perked up. He loved mornings! He scrambled up and over his brothers and sisters.

Spunky had so many things to do—there was paper to play with,

things to investigate,

and pillows to wrestle.

But most important . . .

. . . breakfast!

Oh no! There was no room for him at the red plastic food bowl. Push, shove, still no room.

Desperate and hungry, Spunky jumped over everyone. Right into the middle of the bowl. *Whew!*

3

With a full tummy, Spunky was ready for new adventures. He found a great place to hide.

Then he played chase with the big gray cat, Samantha. She didn't like puppies sneaking up on her!

He even helped the postman
deliver the mail in a brand-new way.

That night Spunky's mama
taught the tired puppies an important lesson.

"My darlings, there is a time in every pup's life when you
get a new master. Show him respect, and he will depend
on you as much as you depend on him."

The next day Mr. and Mrs. Dobson and their young son, Mark, arrived to adopt one of them.

Mark raced over to the bouncing puppies and inspected them one by one. Spunky tried very hard to be chosen. He wiggled his chubby little body. He pleaded with his soft brown eyes. He drenched Mark's face with wet kisses. And it worked!

Spunky had found himself a master and was off on a new adventure!

It didn't take Spunky long to settle into his new life with his master. He had his favorite digging spots in the garden and a neighborhood filled with wonderful and interesting people.

Soon the last of the fall leaves fell to the ground.

Mark taught Spunky to stay, sit, and heel.

Spunky's reward was a trip to a farm
full of strange smells and lots of
exciting animals to meet.

Mark said his prayers that night, thanking his Master for the wonderful day. Spunky finally understood that Mark had a Master he depended on, too!

Tired but content, Spunky and Mark climbed into the bed and happily snuggled together for the night.

The days grew shorter and colder. One morning Spunky peeked out the frost-covered window. There were huge piles of fluffy snow everywhere!

Wow! Snow!

Dodge to the right! Leap to the left! Spunky chased the snowballs Mark threw.

Poof! A snowball exploded right in his face!

13

Spunky and Mark raced down the steep hill on Mark's round sled. *Whoooosh . . . BUMP!* Spunky and Mark flew up in the air, off the sled . . .

. . . and landed, *SPLAT,* face first in the snow.

Covered with snow, Mark exclaimed, "Christmas is almost here, Spunky! Christmas is when we celebrate the birthday of Jesus. The best part of Christmas is the pageant, when they retell the Bible story and have live animals and everything right in church."

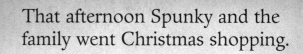

That afternoon Spunky and the family went Christmas shopping.

After putting all the presents in the cab of their truck, there was no room left for Spunky.

Mark opened the back of the truck. "Up you go," encouraged Mark.

The truck doors closed, and the Dobsons started off for home.

Suddenly the tailgate of the truck fell open!

Eyes round with terror, Spunky slid off the back of the truck. He landed in the middle of a busy intersection full of honking horns and squealing tires!

SEASONS GREETIN

He froze. There was a row of huge tires coming right for him!

Spunky crouched in fear as the truck thundered over him.
Panicking, Spunky leaped from the road and ran down the alley.

19

Where was his master?!

Spunky soon came to a junkyard. *A relative must live there*, thought Spunky when he saw the doghouse through the fence.

He crawled through a small hole in the
fence and started to look around.

21

Suddenly he was surrounded by a group of dogs.

"Hey, kid, do you want to spend Christmas with us?" asked one of the dogs.

"That's very kind of you, but I've got to find my master, Mark," Spunky told the dogs.

"There is no master in the junkyard, and we don't need one, either!" growled a mean bulldog as he chased Spunky away.

Yipes!

23

Spunky ran from the junkyard, very confused. Didn't everyone have a master? He knew he needed and wanted *his* master. But how would he find him? Feeling tired and lonely, Spunky rested at the end of a long, dark alley.

He felt a warm light shine on his cold face. Spunky stared up at the window. On it was a picture of a man with a dog and several sheep. He had the kindest face Spunky had seen in a long time.

Spunky tiptoed inside the building to get warm.

25

Lots and lots of people
surrounded Spunky. At the front of the
huge room was a funny-looking barn filled with
children, sheep, chickens, and a cow!

Spunky heard the names Joseph and Mary.
This must be the place Mark told him about!
His Master's house!

Spunky crept closer to watch.

A young girl with angel wings spoke. "When Joseph and Mary arrived in Bethlehem, the time came for her baby to be born. She had a son, Jesus, and laid him in a manger because there was no room for them at the inn."

A boy angel continued. "An angel of the Lord appeared among the shepherds in the fields that night. 'Don't be afraid. I bring you good news of great joy for everyone. The Savior has been born tonight in Bethlehem.'"

Just then Spunky was lifted up and placed on the stage! Together, Spunky and the shepherds listened to the rest of the pageant.

"Glory to God in the highest, and peace on earth to all."

Spunky couldn't help but bark with excitement. The Savior had been born!

A few minutes later, the church door flew open—and in ran Mark!

"Spunky!" he yelled. "I thought we'd lost you! I have been looking for you all night. I was so worried about you. Then I heard you barking as we drove past the church!"

Spunky licked Mark's face with joy. What a wonderful first Christmas!

"I found my master. I'm *so* glad to be home!"

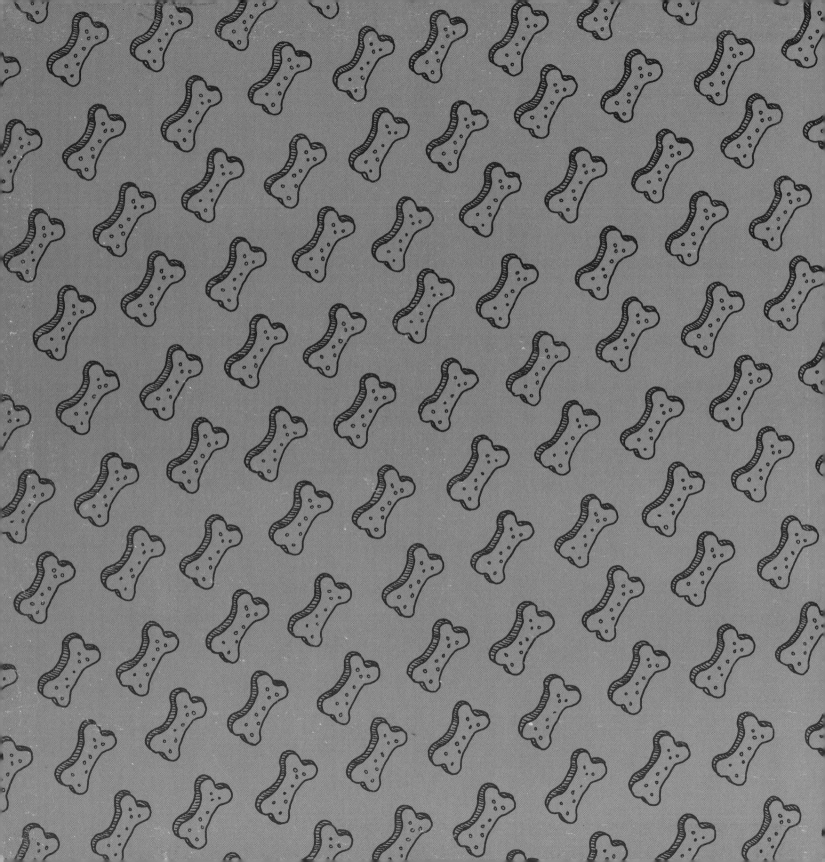